Library of Congress catalog card number: 2006934366
ISBN-10: 0-06-083723-3 — ISBN-13: 978-0-06-083723-5
Book design by John Sazaklis
❖

SPIDER-MAN 3™

THE MOVIE STORYBOOK

ADAPTED BY KATE EGAN

SCREENPLAY BY ALVIN SARGENT

SCREEN STORY BY SAM RAIMI & IVAN RAIMI

BASED ON THE MARVEL COMIC BOOK BY STAN LEE AND STEVE DITKO

HarperEntertainment
An Imprint of HarperCollins Publishers

Peter Parker was on top of the world. Everything was going his way! He was acing his college classes. Mary Jane, or M.J. to her friends, was finally his girlfriend. And his alter ego, Spider-Man, was New York City's hero!

Everyone knew the city was a safer place with Spider-Man fighting crime. There was even a bright new sign in Times Square, flashing NEW YORK ♥'S SPIDER-MAN! It felt good to be appreciated.

Peter smiled up at it as he hurried by. He was on his way to see M.J. perform in her first Broadway show.

There was one person who *didn't* appreciate him, though. Harry Osborn was angry at Spider-Man for killing his father, the Green Goblin. Now that Harry knew that Spider-Man was really Peter, he was angry at Peter, too.

They used to be best friends, and Peter was upset that Harry believed Spider-Man had killed the Green Goblin. But there was no talking to Harry. He just wouldn't listen.

Peter sighed. If it weren't for Harry, his life would be perfect.

That night, after M.J.'s show, Peter took her on a long bike ride beyond the city lights. They watched a beautiful meteor shower in the sky.

Peter was so happy that he forgot all about Harry Osborn. He also didn't notice the mysterious black goo that oozed from a meteorite crater nearby. The goo traveled across the field, and onto Peter's shoe.

Things were going so well with M.J. that Peter told Aunt May he wanted to marry Mary Jane!

"Marriage means years of responsibility," Aunt May warned him. She also pointed out that Peter didn't have a full-time job yet. Peter was sure he could handle it.

The next morning, M.J. showed up at Peter's apartment, disappointed in the newspaper reviews of her performance. Peter tried to help her feel better, but then he heard a radio call.

There was an accident downtown—and Spider-Man couldn't let anyone down. He needed to be there! Peter was sure he could comfort M.J. later.

A wayward crane had torn into an office building, smashing
through the windows and interrupting a photo shoot inside an office.
Now the model was hanging out the window by a telephone cord.

Spider-Man to the rescue! He swung in on his web and carried the
model to safety before he realized she was someone he knew: Gwen
Stacy, the police chief's daughter, who sat next to him in school. It
was nice to be able to help a friend.

As usual, the story was big news in the *Daily Bugle* newspaper. But Peter Parker hadn't snapped the front-page photo. This time it was a new photographer named Eddie Brock.

Peter ran into Eddie at the paper's office, where they were both asking J.J. Jameson for a full-time job. The editor yelled, "I want a photographer who'll expose Spider-Man for the crook he really is!" Whoever got the picture would get the job. Suddenly, Peter wasn't the only photographer in town.

That wasn't the only new obstacle in his way. Spider-Man had defeated the Green Goblin, and the man behind the goblin mask, Norman Osborn, was dead. But someone else was now in the goblin lair, inhaling the potent green gas. It was Norman's son, Harry, who had become the New Goblin! He wanted revenge for his father's death.

As Peter left the *Daily Bugle,* the New Goblin swooped in on his Sky-Stick and grabbed him.

"It had to come to this!" the New Goblin growled. Peter was confused until he realized it was Harry underneath the mask.

Once again, Peter insisted that he hadn't killed Harry's father, but the New Goblin didn't believe him and attacked. To defend himself, Peter lured the New Goblin into an alley and made a web trip wire. When the New Goblin's Sky-Stick hit it, he was thrown off and hit the ground headfirst!

The New Goblin was Peter's enemy, but Harry was still his friend. When he realized Harry was hurt, Peter rushed him to the hospital.

Luckily, Harry was fine except for one thing: He had lost some of his memory. He didn't remember blaming Spider-Man for his father's death!

Peter was glad he and Harry could be friends again. As they played basketball at Harry's mansion, Peter noticed Harry's reflexes were still enhanced by the green gas. But Harry didn't remember becoming the New Goblin, and Spider-Man had one less villain to fight . . . at least for now.

In another corner of the city, a convict named Flint Marko broke out of jail. He had to see his daughter, Penny, who was very ill. He sneaked into his family's apartment to see her.

Penny was happy to see him, but Mrs. Marko was still furious that he had become a criminal. She made him leave.

With the police after him, Flint made his way to a deserted marsh. Flint could see their searchlights flashing and hear their barking dogs.

To escape, he climbed over a fence with a sign that read HIGH ENERGY PARTICLE PHYSICS TEST SITE.

Inside the test site, Flint was exposed to a strange bright light. He blacked out.

When he came to his senses, Flint realized something weird had happened. His body was now made out of sand! He was now Sandman.

Flint had to learn how to shape the sand and move again. As soon he got the hang of it, he left the test site, one step ahead of the police.

The next day, thousands of people gathered to watch Spider-Man receive a key to the city. Kids were dressed like Spider-Man, and everyone was chanting his name. It was a giant party in Spider-Man's honor!

After a speech by the mayor, the police chief's daughter, Gwen, introduced Spider-Man to the crowd. He swung in dramatically and accepted his award. He felt very proud.

Then his Spidey sense tingled. A few blocks away, the police had found Flint Marko. Flint outwitted them by jumping into a truck and transforming into a pile of sand. Then he pummeled the officers with his giant sand fists!

Now the sandstorm was raging past the celebration. Spider-Man soared after it on his web, as the sand engulfed an armored truck, punching holes in its roof!

When Spider-Man swooped inside the truck, he found Flint Marko standing there . . . scooping up cash! When Spider-Man's fist went right through him, he realized that the guy and the sand were one and the same. Flint Marko was Sandman.

As Spider-Man and Sandman fought, they broke open the back door of the truck. Spider-Man webbed him to a passing car and clapped the two together, but the web couldn't hold him and Sandman escaped. Spider-Man stopped Sandman from doing more harm . . . but the villain still got away with the cash.

Eddie Brock captured it all in a photo, and J.J. Jameson loved it. It ran on the front page with the headline: SANDMAN! SON OF A BEACH. EVEN SPIDER-MAN CAN'T STOP HIM!

Peter was suddenly upset. He now knew Eddie would get the full-time photographer job.

Peter took Mary Jane to a fancy restaurant that night so he could ask her to marry him. He was nervous and excited.

However, M.J. was still feeling upset about her bad reviews, and she felt like Peter didn't understand. She was so mad that she left dinner before he could pop the question!

To make matters worse, Peter and Aunt May were summoned to the police station. The police wanted to talk about who had killed Uncle Ben. There was a new suspect, and he was still on the loose.

Thinking about Uncle Ben made Peter angry. What good were his spider-powers if they hadn't saved his uncle?

Now that things weren't going well, Peter was hard on himself. Even M.J. was worried. The next time she saw him, she said, "We all need help some-times, Peter. Even Spider-Man."

He didn't want to hear it, though. Nothing could snap him out of his bad mood. His job, his friendships, and his future were all on the line.

He didn't realize it yet, but something else was getting him down. Since his bike trip with Mary Jane, the strange black goo had been hiding in his apartment. While Peter was sleeping, it oozed all over him and gave him a nightmare!

When he woke up, Peter was clinging to a skyscraper in a new black spider suit! It felt different from his red-and-blue suit. Spider-Man felt stronger, more powerful. As if nothing could stand in his way. He took off through the city.

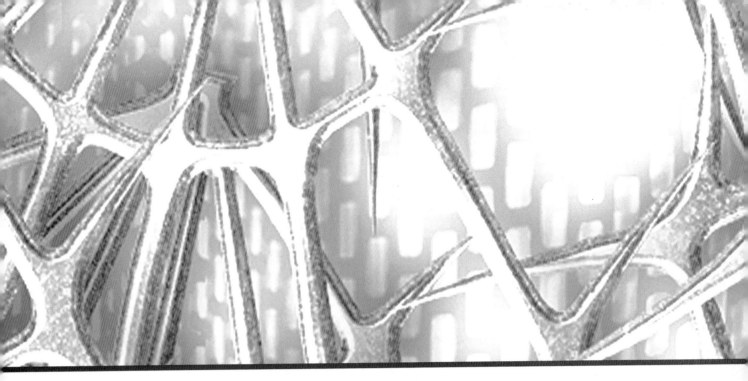

Spider-Man swung in to catch a petty thief. He happened to see Eddie Brock snapping a picture, and Spider-Man smashed his camera! It felt good to stop the crime, and even better to stop Eddie. In the black suit, Spider-Man wasn't afraid to show his anger.

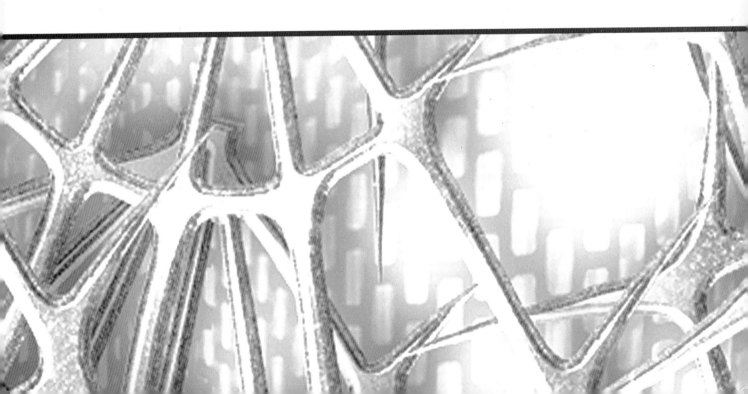

Spider-Man came across Sandman in a subway tunnel, carrying stolen cash from another bank robbery. He wasn't going to get away this time! Spider-Man knocked him to the tracks, and then slung a web to the pipes overhead. When he tore them down, water flooded into the tunnel—and turned Sandman into mud! It was another victory for the new Spider-Man.

When he returned home, Peter's landlord asked for the rent. It was a simple question, but Peter yelled at him. He couldn't control his rage.

Shaken, Peter returned to his apartment and looked in the mirror. A terrifying black figure stared back at him for an instant before he averted his eyes. All of a sudden Peter realized something: Wearing the black suit was dangerous.

Peter could tell it made him more powerful, but also more reckless. He stuffed the suit in a box and pushed it to the back of his closet.

He noticed some black goo on his floor. It looked strange, and he sent it away to be tested at a lab.

The next day, Peter headed to Central Park to see M.J. again. He wanted to make things work.

It didn't go well, though. M.J. was still mad, and she didn't want to talk to him.

Hurt, Peter thought only one thing could cheer him up. He put the black suit on underneath his clothes. His fears and sadness disappeared at once.

Walking down the street, he spotted the front page of the *Daily Bugle*. SPIDER-MAN IS A THIEF! it read. Beside the story was a phony photo. Peter knew Eddie Brock had to be behind it!

Peter stormed into the *Bugle* offices and exposed the photo as a fake. J.J. Jameson fired Eddie on the spot! The black suit had worked its magic and one of Peter's foes, at least, was out of his hair.

He went to Harry's mansion next, to see how his friend was doing. Peter soon realized Harry's memory was back, and he was the New Goblin again!

The New Goblin wanted to finish what he started. He threw a pumpkin bomb at Peter. Under attack, Peter didn't think twice. He grabbed another pumpkin bomb and threw it right in the New Goblin's face! With the black suit on, Peter felt only the faintest twinge of guilt about what he had done to his friend.

Soon after, Dr. Connors, the scientist who had tested the sample of black goo, contacted Peter with the results. The stuff was alive, Dr. Connors explained. It manipulated its host like a parasite. He advised Peter to steer clear of it. It was dangerous.

Peter didn't listen to the warning. Instead, he went to Aunt May's and bragged that he could track down Uncle Ben's killer. Nobody would ever escape from him like that again.

Aunt May surprised him with her reaction. She missed Uncle Ben every day, but she had no dreams of getting back at his killer.

"Don't live with revenge in your heart," she begged Peter. "It turns you into something ugly."

Inside his new black suit, though, Peter could hardly hear what she was saying. The black goo was slowly transforming him into someone else.

The bad reviews had cost Mary Jane her part in the show, and she was now singing in a jazz club. Peter decided to go and make her jealous by taking Gwen Stacy as his date.

When Gwen saw M.J. onstage, though, she realized Peter was using her and left in a huff. M.J. was furious, too. Peter lashed out at her and made an embarrassing scene!

Peter was so angry that he shoved M.J. out of his way. Then he stopped and realized that something was terribly wrong. He saw M.J.'s tearful face. He glanced out the window and saw his friend Gwen stalking away, angry.

What have I done? Peter wondered. M.J. was right. He did need help. He decided to help himself by taking the black suit off once and for all. Peter went into the night by himself.

Peter slipped into the bell tower of a church,
where he was sure to be alone.

The black suit clung to his body, like it wanted to stay there, but Peter struggled to peel it off piece by piece. When the church bells began to ring, something amazing happened. The goo just melted away! Peter felt clean and fresh without the black stuff on his skin. He was ready to make a new start. But he wasn't the only one. . . .

One of the people in the church was Eddie Brock, praying for Peter to get what he deserved. Eddie hated Peter for getting him fired.

When the black goo melted off Peter, it dripped down onto Eddie. In his fury, Eddie sensed its dark power. It rained onto his hands, soaking into his skin.

Looking up, Eddie saw that Peter was really Spider-Man, but there was no time to think about that. When Eddie opened his mouth, a drop of the goo fell on his tongue . . . transforming him into a monstrous creature called Venom!

Venom was born with one consuming urge: to get revenge. He began to form a plan, and it involved Sandman.

Feeling guilty, Peter set off for Harry's mansion. Harry was not ready to forgive Peter. As they argued, a live TV broadcast came on.

Venom and Sandman were at a construction site, guarding their hostage: Mary Jane! The two villains were waiting for Spider-Man. Venom's black web taunted SPIDER-MAN—STOP US IF YOU CAN!

Peter turned to Harry. "I can't take on them both," he said humbly.

Harry had enough New Goblin power to help. But there was no way he was helping his father's killer! Harry threw Peter out of his house.

Later, though, Harry's butler confirmed what Peter had told him. Spider-Man really hadn't killed the Green Goblin. Harry's father had died by his own hand.

Spider-Man soared to the construction site alone, and Venom lunged for him.

"I want to humiliate you on live TV," Venom cackled, "with the help of my friend, Sandman."

Peter saw M.J. struggling in Venom's web, but he couldn't get to her now. Sandman's massive hands kept crashing together, smashing him. The two were a fearsome team. And then the New Goblin blazed in!

Spider-Man, Sandman, Venom, and the New Goblin battled fiercely as a crowd gathered to watch. "It's the end of Spider-Man," someone shouted. Peter was starting to wonder if that was true.

Just then, Sandman got distracted, and Spider-Man rescued M.J. As he turned to fight Venom, he noticed Venom flinching with every clang of the steel girders at the construction site. The vibrations were hurting the black goo that formed his suit!

Spider-Man tried to persuade Eddie Brock to give up the Venom suit. But Eddie loved the power too much.

So Spider-Man clanged metal pipes until the sounds grew too loud for Venom to withstand. Then he knocked the monster down! Black goo oozed from Venom's wounds, then sizzled and evaporated until only a single drop remained.

Venom was defeated, and so was Peter's urge for revenge. He'd loved the powerful feeling from the black suit, but now he knew that it could destroy him.

From now on, Spider-Man would have to find his strength elsewhere. In justice and peace. In family and forgiveness. And in M.J., who was ready to give him another chance.